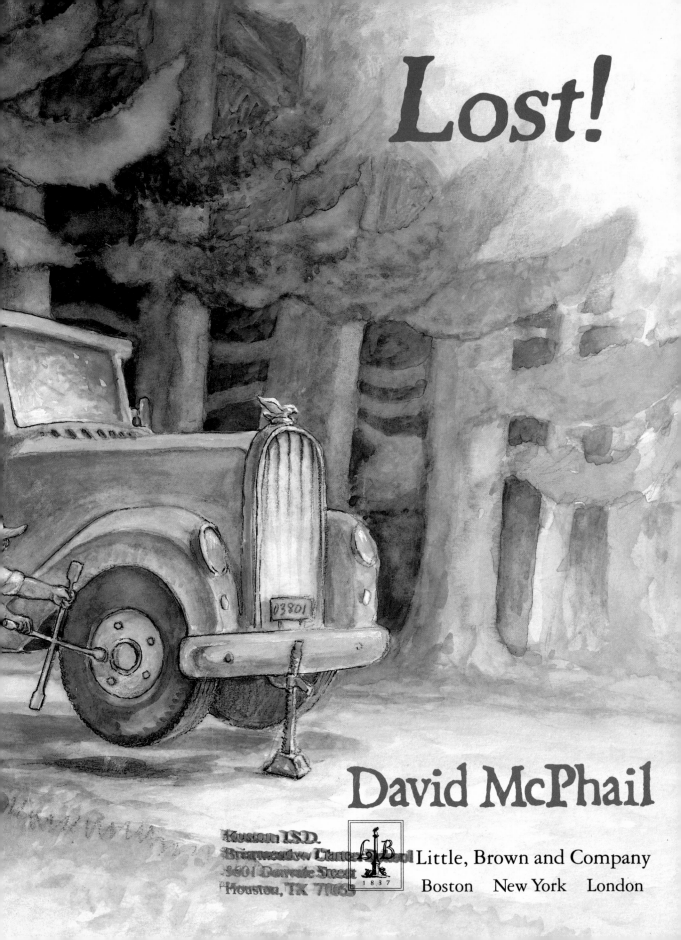

Lost!

David McPhail

Little, Brown and Company

Boston   New York   London

For Kiko and for Dutch,
who would be lost without him.

Books by David McPhail

Santa's Book of Names
Lost!
Something Special
First Flight
Andrew's Bath
The Bear's Toothache
The Train
Henry Bear's Park

First Paperback Edition

Library of Congress Cataloging-in-Publication Data

McPhail, David M.
  Lost! / David McPhail. — 1st ed.
    p.   cm.
  Summary: On his way to school, a small boy befriends a
very large bear who is lost.
  ISBN 0-316-56329-3 (hc)
  ISBN 0-316-56336-6 (pb)
  [1. Lost children—Fiction.   2. Bears—Fiction.]   I. Title.
PZ7.M2427Lp   1990
[E]—dc19   88-22663

10 9

WOR
Printed in the United States of America

I am walking down the street when I hear
someone crying.

It's a bear!

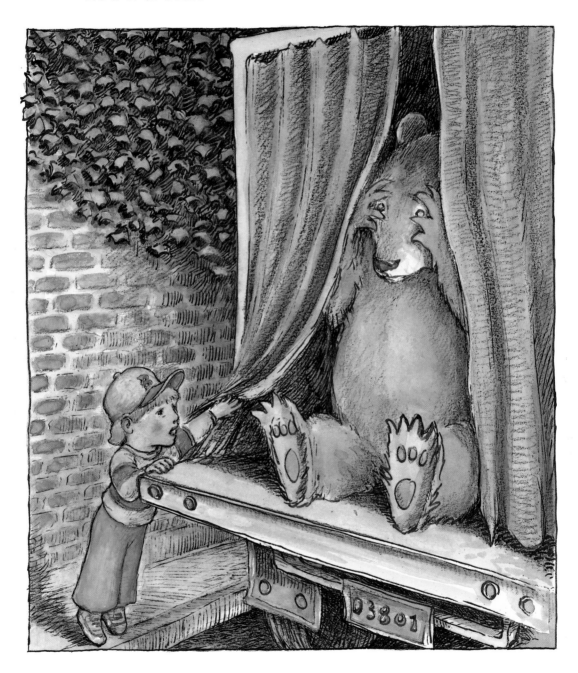

He looks lost and afraid.
The tall buildings scare him.
And he's never seen so many people.

"Don't worry," I tell him.
"The buildings won't hurt you,
and most of the people are friendly."

"How did you get here?" I ask.
"I climbed in to have a nap," he explains,
"and when I woke up, I was *lost!*"

"I'll help you. Tell me where you live."

"There are trees where I live," he tells me.
So we find some trees.

"More trees," he says, "and water!"

I take him to a place where there are more trees —
and water, too.

"No," he says. "This is not it either."

I have an idea.
"Follow me!" I say.

I take him to a tall building.

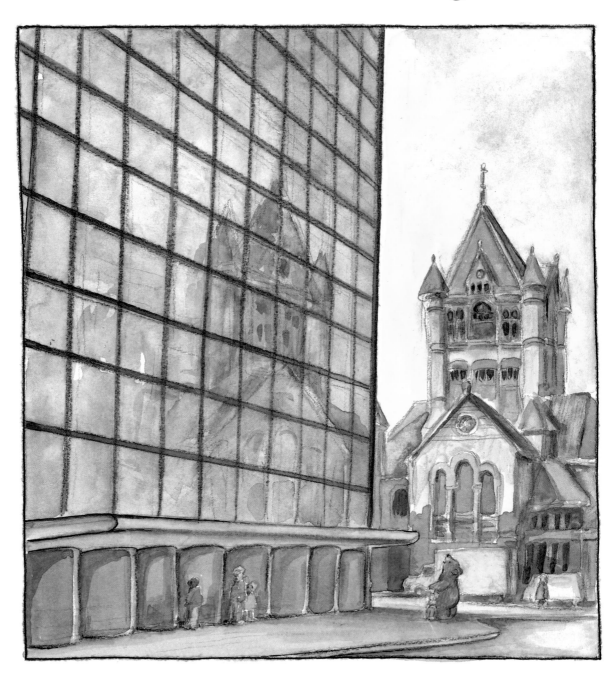

We go inside, get on the elevator,
and ride all the way to the top.

From up here we can see the whole city.
"Look!" I say. "Now we can find your home."
"There it is!" he says, pointing.

Down we go, across three streets
and into the park.

The park is not the bear's home after all —

but he likes it there.

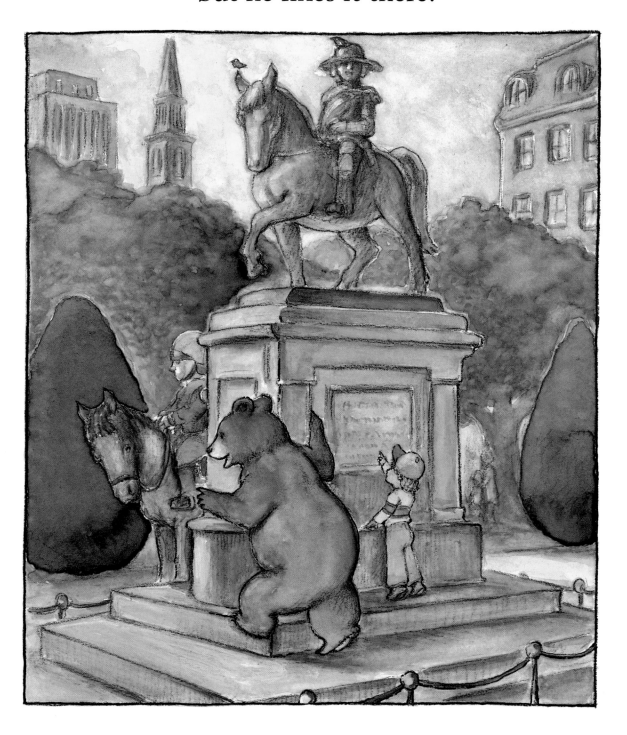

We go for a boat ride,

we have lunch,

and we go to the playground.

We are having a good time.

But it is getting late, and the bear is still lost.

"Let's try the library," I tell him.
"We can find out anything here!"

Inside the library we look through lots of books.
The bear sees a picture that looks like his home.

We find the place on a map

and hurry outside.

A bus is leaving.

We get on the bus and ride for a long time.

Finally, we are there.

"*This* is where I live!" says the bear.

He gives me a hug and thanks me again for my help.

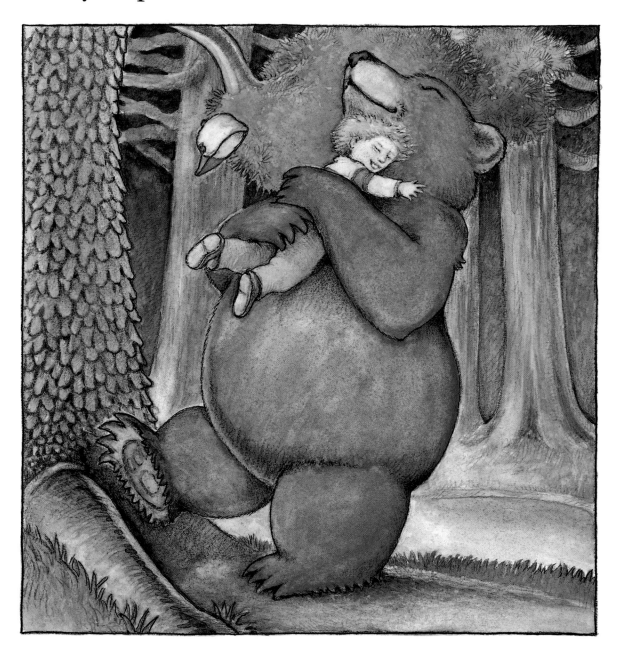

Then he waves good-bye and disappears into the forest.

The trees are so tall, and there aren't any people.

"Wait!" I call to the bear, "come back!

"I think I'm lost!" I tell him.

"Don't worry," he says.

"I will help you."